Gathering the Glimmers

Written and Illustrated by Ffion Jones

TINY TREE

Gathering the Glimmers
Published in 2025 by
Tiny Tree Books
West Wing Studios
Unit 166, The Mall
Luton, LU1 2TL
tinytreebooks.com

Copyright © 2025 Ffion Jones

The right of Ffion Jones to be identified as author of this work has been asserted in accordance with the Copyright, Designs and Patents Act 1988.

All rights reserved. No reproduction, copy or transmission of this publication may be made without express prior written permission. No paragraph of this publication may be reproduced, copied or transmitted except with express prior written permission or in accordance with the provisions of the Copyright Act 1956 (as amended). Any person who commits any unauthorised act in relation to this publication may be liable to criminal prosecution and civil claims for damage.

All characters appearing in this work are fictitious. Any resemblance to real persons, living or dead, is purely coincidental.

Wren's steps are slow and heavy.
Twigs snap under her feet. The forest
is a spidery web shutting out the light.

Staring at the shadows twisting all around her,
Wren feels her tummy doing loop-de-loops.
"What if there is no way out?"
"What if I can't get home?"
"What if I've gone the wrong way?"

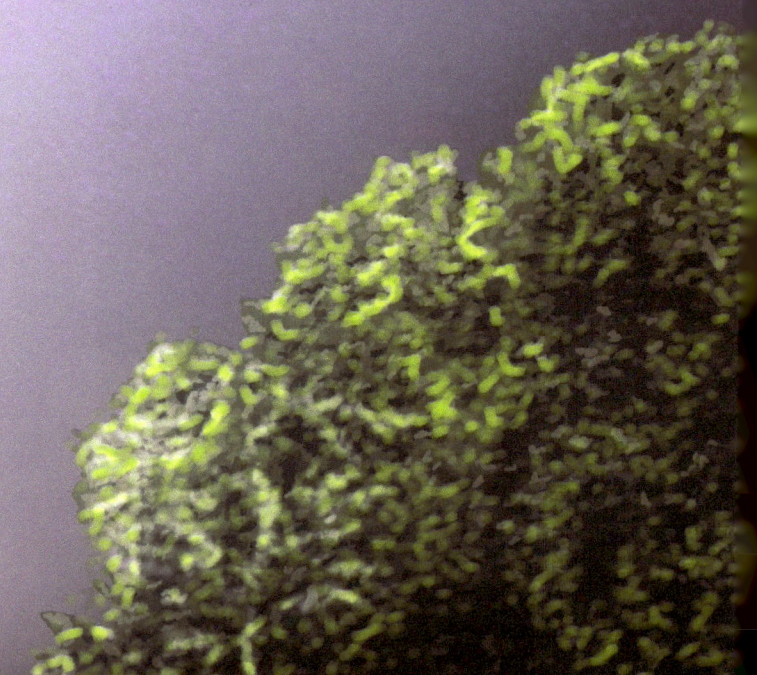

Wren's heart starts pounding and her muscles tense. All she can smell is fear. She bites her lip as she climbs through the brambles, sharp like thorns.

Wren walks deeper into the tangle of trees, but still she can't see the way through. The path is growing darker and home seems so far away.

With each corner Wren turns, the more her worries grow.
"What if night falls?"
"What if danger lies in wait?"
"What if I'm left all alone?"
The "what ifs" fill her head and freeze her to the spot.
Time slows to a crawl and the world starts to spin.

There is nothing Wren can do but stop.
Rooted like the branches beside her,
she takes a slow breath.

When Wren breathes in deeply, the air is rich with the scent of damp bark. As she listens closely, she can hear the trees hum. Is the forest full only of darkness, or is there something else? Wren watches and waits.

The blackest of crows hops onto a branch,
filling the air with its croaks and caws.
Steady for a moment, it then shifts back and forth,
finally diving into the woods, whistling its song.

A copper-coloured leaf pirouettes from the sky, dancing to the rhythm of the wind: to the left and to the right, twirling like confetti.
Another leaf, burnt orange, meets it mid-air.
They swirl and fall together like petals of snow.

Wren lifts her face and sees the smallest glint of light.
Has it been there all along?

As Wren watches the leaves dancing to the tiny glimmers of light, something warms inside her. She remembers the winter sun and playing snowballs on the hills, her breath like dragons' smoke in the cold, clear air.

Though still deep in the forest, Wren now feels safe and calm. She knows that the glimmers are inside of her too.

Wren's steps are quick and easy. Twigs crunch under her feet like crisp snow. The forest is a beautiful web of life welcoming the light.

Wren looks at the glimmers shimmering
all around her and her heart sings.